# Nose Grows
## Jonathan Allen

ORCHARD BOOKS

ORCHARD BOOKS
96 Leonard Street, London EC2A 4RH
Orchard Books Australia
14 Mars Road, Lane Cove, NSW 2066
ISBN 1 85213 637 5 (hardback)
ISBN 1 85213 986 2 (paperback)
First published in Great Britain 1994
First paperback publication 1995
© Jonathan Allen 1994
The right of Jonathan Allen to be identified as the author and illustrator
of this work has been asserted by him in accordance with the Copyright,
Designs and Patents Act, 1988.
A CIP catalogue record for this book is available from the British Library.
Printed in Great Britain

# Contents

# Growing Pains

A long time ago there lived a very famous and very accomplished wizard called Grimweed. He was so well thought of that his services were in huge demand throughout the kingdom and far beyond. His speciality was potions. Because of this, he had become known as "The Mighty Grimweed, King of Potions", and people travelled great distances to consult him.

People such as King Wo of Wiwaxia, for instance, who with his royal procession was slowly approaching Magic City, bringing with

him his own very special problem. (New readers' note: Magic City is the name of Grimweed's home and magic laboratory.)

King Wo liked to travel in style, with a long procession of servants and bodyguards. This time he seemed to have even more than usual. At the head of the procession there was the Royal Herald. Then came The King's Own Royal Bodyguard, followed by a line of elaborately dressed servants walking slowly and carefully, holding cushions at shoulder level.

Immediately after them, seated on his special portable travelling throne, which was carried by four more servants, came King Wo himself.

Well, when I say "after" them, this is not strictly true. He was — how shall I put it? — in front of them, amongst them and behind them all at the same time. You see, what the servants were carrying so carefully on their cushions was the King's nose. . . four metres of it.

Grimweed watched their approach from his special observation turret.

"This should be interesting," he said to himself. "I've heard of following your nose, but this is ridiculous!" He chuckled as he made his way down the stone steps to the Magic Laboratory.

"Lloyd," he said, poking his head round the door. "Do you think you could join me in the consulting room in a couple of minutes, please? I'm going to need some assistance."

"Something big come up?" inquired Lloyd.

"Yes, you could say that," replied Grimweed, with a grin. "Well, something long anyway!"

The consulting room was in turmoil by the time Grimweed and Lloyd got there. King Wo's servants were trying to manoeuvre his portable travelling throne through the narrow doorway without causing too much nasal distress to His Majesty the King.

Servants and guards were cursing and tripping over one another while the King shouted instructions at them between yells of pain.

"Back a bit, back a bit, OW! What are you doing, you idiot? No! No, it won't bend round like that! . . . Careful with that spear! AAARGH!"

"Your Majesty!" cried Grimweed, taking control of the situation. "Perhaps if someone could open that window, and perhaps if you could stick some of your nose out of it, you might be able to turn round and come in backwards. Let's try that, shall we? That's it slowly, slowly . . . Ah! There we are!"

With sighs of relief, the servants set the throne down on the stone floor.

"Kings!" thought Grimweed. "Why can't they just walk around like other people?"

"Now, Your Majesty," he said aloud when they had all got their breath back. "I won't ask you what the problem is. I mean, it's pretty obvious what's wrong. In fact you could say it sticks out a mile!"

He nudged the King, who glared at him. "This is no laughing matter," said King Wo coldly. "It's not exactly fun having a nose this long, you know. Especially when you can remember what it used to be like. Let me tell you, in its original state this nose was the talk of the kingdom."

"I should think it still is!" thought Grimweed. "It's got be at least four metres long!"

"My nose," continued the King, "was the noblest, most beautiful nose in the whole of Wiwaxia. The exquisite rounded end, the elegant flare of the nostrils and their perfect width were admired by all. But not any more. Now look at it!"

Grimweed regarded King Wo's nose for
a moment with his head on one side.

"It would be hard not to look at it," he
muttered under his breath.

"You want me to bring it back to its
normal size and shape, is that right?" he
asked the King.

"That was the general idea," said King
Wo.

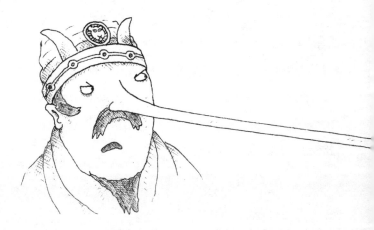

"Right," said Grimweed, in a 'Let's get
on with it' kind of voice. "Let's see exactly
what we're dealing with here, shall we? It's
evidently a spell of some kind. Lloyd, pass me
my wand, will you? Thanks."

Grimweed ushered the servants and
bodyguards out of the way.

"I should imagine it's something fairly
simple," he predicted. "If you all wouldn't
mind standing back we'll just find out . . .
Keep still, Your Majesty."

He stretched out his arm and gently touched the King's nose with his wand. There was a bang, a puff of purple smoke and a yelp of pain from King Wo — and from Grimweed, who dropped his wand as though it were red hot.

"Wow!" said Grimweed, shaking his hand to get the feeling back. "There again, it might not be so simple!"

He turned to the King, who was rubbing his nose, or what he could reach of it.

"I'm sorry, Your Majesty. I had no idea it was going to do that!"

"Was that . . . Was that a protection spell?" asked Lloyd, astonished.

"Yes," replied Grimweed, retrieving his wand. "A protection spell and a half! I have a nasty feeling this is going to get complicated!"

"Hey! That was painful!" cried the King. "My nose has gone all red! I hope it's not damaged."

"You should see my wand," retorted Grimweed, ruefully examining its smoke-blackened end. "Now that's painful!" He shook his head. "Your Majesty, this is serious magic. What on earth have you been doing? You haven't offended any Grand Wizards recently, have you?"

"No," said King Wo. "I have great respect for wizards."

"Very wise," said Grimweed, "but there's someone out there who doesn't like you, and who certainly knows their way round a magic wand. Have you offended any Grand Witches recently?"

"Witches?" cried the King in disgust. "I don't bother myself with witches! I wouldn't stoop so low! . . . Oooh! Urgh! Oh no! It's growing again!"

Grimweed raised one eyebrow.

"Lloyd," he said, "take the end of this tape-measure and line it up with the tip of the King's nose, will you? I'm going to conduct a little experiment. If anything, er . . . occurs, let me know. OK? Now, Your Majesty, what was that about witches?"

"They're the lowest of the low!" cried King Wo. "Ow! Oooh! Ah! It's happening again!"

"Three centimetres!" cried Lloyd. "Which takes it up to four metres fifteen."

"So you don't like witches?" Grimweed asked.

"I hate them!" replied the King. "Ah! Eurgh!"

"Four metres eighteen!" called Lloyd, from the other end of the King's nose.

"As I suspected," said Grimweed. "It's a 'Nose Grows' spell."

"A 'Nose Grows' spell?" echoed King Wo.

"Tell his majesty about 'Nose Grows'

spells, will you, Lloyd?" said Grimweed.

"A 'Nose Grows' spell," began Lloyd, "is a spell which causes the victim's nose to grow a set distance — in your case, three centimetres — whenever a certain set of circumstances occur. In this example, it seems to happen every time you say

something bad about a witch. And, from your present nasal length, I would estimate that you seriously offended a very powerful witch twenty days ago, or thereabouts."

King Wo was outraged.

"A witch?" he cried. "A common witch dares to put a spell on me, the King of Wiwaxia?" His voice rose. "A disgusting witch dares to put a spell on my beautiful nose? A thousand curses on all wi . . .!"

"Your Majesty!" cried Grimweed, lunging forward and clapping his hand over the king's mouth just in time. "At three centimetres per curse," he warned, "I suggest you watch what you say, unless you want your nose to arrive home two hours before the rest of you."

King Wo breathed deeply.

"All right," he said at last. "Point taken. A curse on all w-wallabies, w-watering cans and w-w-wigwams."

"Well," said Grimweed, "we may not know which witch, or why, but at least we've got a good idea where. In which case, Your Majesty, we should make our way to Wiwaxia as soon as possible."

"But I've just come all the way here!" cried King Wo.

"Your Majesty," explained Grimweed, "with that protection spell around it, there's not a lot I, or anyone else, can do about your nose. I'm afraid that the only person who can take the 'Nose Grows' spell off with any degree of safety is the one who put it on in the first place."

"And that person is back in Wiwaxia!" groaned the King.

The journey to Wiwaxia was not uneventful. The King's nose grew by at least half a metre in the space of the first fifty kilometres, a large part of this growth occurring when he insisted that a carriage-load of priestesses on their way to the holy shrine of Snatto the Brave should leave the road to let him through. The priestesses objected, so The King's Own Royal Bodyguard simply pushed them out of the way.

Grimweed and Lloyd sat in the back of the carriage and tried to pretend it was nothing to do with them, but it was very embarrassing.

"How many priestesses were there?" Lloyd asked Grimweed, once they were a safe distance away.

"Five," he replied, "and King Wo's nose grew sixty centimetres."

"I know, but they were priestesses not witches," said Lloyd, puzzled.

"It must be a more general spell," Grimweed reasoned. "His nose grows when he's unpleasant to women generally, not just witches."

"You were right," said Lloyd. "This is getting complicated."

"Tell me, King Wo," asked Grimweed. "Do you often push women out of your way?"

"Only if they are stupid enough not to move of their own accord!" sneered the King. "Women are inferior beings and must stand aside when I approach. Ow! Aagh! Oooh!"

Grimweed looked at Lloyd and rolled his eyes heavenwards.

"I can see how a witch might find that a bit hard to take!" he muttered.

"Four metres eighty-one!" Lloyd mouthed at him.

King Wo was in a permanent bad mood. He sat on his portable travelling throne and fumed.

"When I get back home I'm going to round up every witch I can find, and cast them out of the kingdom!" he raged. "Ow! Ooooh!"

"Four metres eighty-four," counted Lloyd. "Try to calm down, Your Majesty."

The King snorted.

"So what's Wiwaxia like?" Lloyd asked Grimweed.

"It's a nice place," he replied, "when you get to know it. When I was a student I spent the summer holidays in Wiwax City at my Aunt Jocasta's house with her and her daughter Gloria. Gloria was at Magic School with me." Grimweed laughed. "She didn't stand for the 'women are inferior' stuff either.

She didn't need to, she was good. She was studying to be a Grand Witch . . . Ah!"

"You don't think?" said Lloyd.

"I do think!" said Grimweed. He turned to King Wo.

"You haven't come across a large, imposing woman wearing a long red dress with yellow stars on it, by any chance, have you?" he asked. "She's, er . . a friend of my cousin," he lied.

"I pay very little attention to these things, Grimweed," replied the King. "But I do remember a fat woman in an awful starry red dress, now that you mention it. She refused to get out of the road, so my men threw her in the town pond. We had a good laugh about that! It was a couple of weeks ago, I think. Ow! Ooooh! Eeeurgh!"

35

"You threw her in the pond?" repeated Grimweed slowly, as though he couldn't quite believe it. He looked at Lloyd, raised his eyebrows and shook his head in wonder.

"Four metres eighty-seven!" whispered Lloyd.

"Well, that's who and why sorted out," said Grimweed quietly, still shaking his head in disbelief.

"Here we are," said Grimweed, ducking beneath a metal sign with the letter "G" painted on it in red surrounded by yellow stars. "Aunt Jocasta's, and by the looks of that sign, Gloria's living here now. Let's go in and see if we're right."

He was in one of the tiny back streets of Wiwax City behind the palace. This was where he had stayed when he was a magic student and, as far as he could see, it hadn't changed at all. His reverie was shattered by a delighted shriek.

"Well, look who it isn't!"

A large, imposing woman wearing a long red dress with yellow stars on it bounced up to him and gave him a big hug.

"The Mighty Trevor Wilson!*"

She laughed. "I'm sorry, I can't be doing with this Grimweed stuff. You'll always be my little Trevor to me!"

* Trevor Wilson is Grimweed's real name

"Gloria!" smiled Grimweed, "It is really wonderful to see you! You're looking great!"

"Grand Witch Gloria D'estelle to you, matey!" she corrected him. Grimweed whistled.

"I hear you put all that research into potions to good use," she continued. "King of Potions indeed! My little Trevor!"

Behind him, Lloyd coughed self-consciously.

"Er, this is Lloyd, my assistant," said Grimweed, embarrassed. "Lloyd, this is Grand Witch Gloria D'estelle. When we were at Magic School, Gloria was studying spells while I was studying potions."

"Nice to meet you Lloyd," said Gloria. "Now, what brings you here in your big, pointy hat, little Trevor?"

"Well," said Grimweed, with a twinkle in his eye, "I heard you'd been doing, er . . . a bit of swimming . . . in the town pond, I believe."

"Uh huh," said Gloria, not giving anything away, "and who told you that?"

"Oh, just some King or other," replied Grimweed. "You might know him, he's got a big nose . . . a very big nose."

Gloria grinned. "How long is it now?" she asked.

"Five metres eight centimetres!" replied Lloyd, "as of ten o'clock this morning. He shouted at his maidservants."

"Tremendous!" said Gloria approvingly. "That'll teach him to respect women a bit more! Not to mention witches."

"Yes," admitted Grimweed. "He does have a bit of an attitude problem in those areas, to say the least. Why does he dislike witches so much?"

Gloria snorted. "He thinks that magic is men's business. And that women can't do it properly, and shouldn't be doing it anyway."

Grimweed gave a hollow laugh. "That's what is known as 'asking for trouble'," he said.

"And he's had a grudge against women," she continued, "ever since the girls at school laughed at him because he started wearing a special jewelled nose guard to protect himself when playing football. It didn't half look silly!"

"So you put the 'Nose Grows' spell on him to teach him a lesson and make him change his ways, was that it?"

"That was the idea," replied Gloria.

"Why didn't you just turn him into something unpleasant on the spot?" asked Grimweed.

"He was something unpleasant already!" exclaimed Gloria. "And he was so vain about that hooter of his! I wanted to get him where it would really hurt. He'd been asking for it, Trevor, and when he had me thrown in the pond, that was the last straw!"

Grimweed sighed.

"I wish I hadn't promised to help him now," he groaned. "How long will his nose get before you decide that he's learnt his lesson?"

Gloria shook her head.

"It's not that sort of spell Trevor," she explained. "I don't decide anything. It's up to the King. The solution is built into the spell itself. Which means he can get his nose back to normal size without extra magic. In fact, that's the only way he can, with that protection spell in force."

Grimweed shuddered.

"Don't remind me!" he groaned. "It nearly took my arm off!"

Gloria grinned.

"Like they told us at Magic School. If you're going to do a spell, make it strong!"

She regarded Grimweed and Lloyd's downcast faces for a moment.

"Look, you couple of long-faced wizards, you!" she chided them. "If you really want to help King Wo, help him to help himself. Don't wave your wand at the problem, use what's under your pointy hat, and think. It's really quite obvious, you know!"

Grimweed and Lloyd said goodbye to Gloria and trudged back to the palace in dejected silence, each doing what Gloria had advised, thinking hard. They were feeling useless and not a little foolish. Suddenly Lloyd stopped with an anguished cry.

"Tshah! Idiot!" he cried. "Of course!"

Grimweed looked at him.

"If you've just discovered the blindingly obvious solution, the one that's built into the original spell," he groaned, "I'm going to be very embarrassed."

"Er . . . You're going to be very embarrassed," said Lloyd.

Once back at the palace, they hurried up to the King's chamber to tell him the good news.

"Your problems are over," cried Grimweed, as they burst into the room.

"Lloyd, tell His Majesty what you've just told me!"

Lloyd stepped forward.

"As Your Majesty is aware," he began, "when you say something nasty about a woman, your nose grows three centimetres."

"I hardly need reminding of that," growled the King.

"Well, Your Majesty," Lloyd went on, "the reverse is also true. Every time you say something nice about a woman your nose will shrink three centimetres!" He paused for effect.

King Wo looked sceptical, and not a little annoyed.

"All right, let's conduct an experiment," suggested Grimweed. "Your Majesty, say something nice about a woman . . . Go on, er . . . what about your darling mother?"

"She's an old bat!" said King Wo sulkily.

"Your grandmother?" suggested Grim-weed.

"Granny was all right, I suppose," said the King, grudgingly. Grimweed turned to Lloyd.

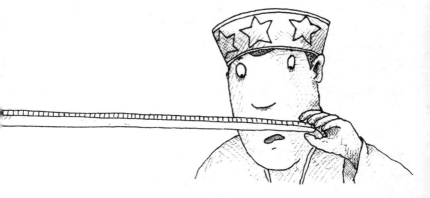

"Anything?" he asked. At the pointy end of the King's nose Lloyd shook his head.

"Too half-hearted," he complained.

"Can't you think of anything nice to say about any woman?" implored Grimweed.

"No!" said the King, sulking even more.

"Right" said Grimweed grimly.

"Lloyd, come with me!"

"Where are we going?" asked Lloyd as Grimweed hurried down the stairs to the kitchen regions.

"To the kitchen," said Grimweed, through gritted teeth. "There's a potion I want to make up, and boy, does the King need it!"

Once in the kitchen, Grimweed comandeered half the big table and took out his Grimproductz emergency potion pack.

"This should have everything we need in it," he said to Lloyd. "See if they've got any honey, will you? Oh, and a glass of beer. No, the beer's nothing to do with the potion, it's for me!"

As Lloyd and an admiring crowd of kitchen staff watched, Grimweed mixed the special ingredients expertly, shook the bottle and held it up to the light.

"OK," he said. "Is any one of you lot taking a drink or suchlike up to the king in the next half-hour?"

"I am," said a maid called Miriam. "I take a glass of sherry to His Majesty at about this time every day."

"Good," said Grimweed. "Put three drops of this stuff in it and take it up to him as normal. Lloyd, let's go back upstairs and see what happens."

"Was it what I think it was?" asked Lloyd, as they climbed the stairs back to the King's chamber. "Some kind of 'Mr Nice Guy' potion?"

"Spot on," said Grimweed. "Maybe now we can get that nose down a bit."

King Wo was still in a sulk when Grimweed and Lloyd entered the room. His nose was propped on its special Royal Nose support, which was a series of poles on stands with cushions on the top. His arms were folded grumpily, and he was breathing heavily.

There was a knock on the door.

"Enter," said the King. The maid came in bearing a glass of sherry on a golden tray.

The King took it without looking at her, knocked back the sherry and banged the glass back down on to the tray.

Grimweed signalled Miriam to stay in the room for a minute. He counted up to ten and then cleared his throat.

"Er, wasn't that a nice glass of sherry?" he inquired.

The King looked at him in surprise.

"Jolly nice!" he agreed. "There's nothing like a glass of sherry in the afternoon I always say!"

"Don't you think Miriam is looking pretty today, Your Majesty," asked Grimweed, indicating the nervous-looking maid. The King turned to look at her. He smiled.

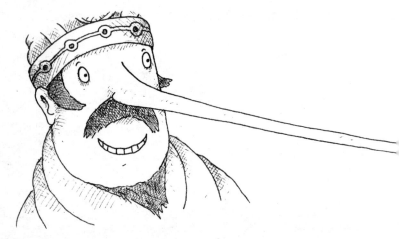

Grimweed winked at Lloyd. The potion was working.

"Watch the end of his nose," he whispered.

"Why yes," said the King. "You look very pretty today, Miriam."

At his post at the end of the King's nose, Lloyd made a thumbs up sign, and raised three fingers to indicate that the King's nose had shrunk by three centimetres. His theory was correct!

Grimweed heaved a sigh of relief.

"Such a lovely name, 'Miriam'," the King was saying. "Don't you think so, Grimweed? I'm so sorry I shouted at you this morning, Miriam. I insist that you take the rest of the day off to make up for your distress."

"That's nine centimetres less," whispered Lloyd. "You should try taking this stuff, Grimweed. I could do with a holiday!"

"Shush!" said Grimweed, giving him a nudge. "We've got some work to do!"

He turned to the King.

"Tell me about your grandmother, Your Majesty. . . " he prompted.

"A wonderful woman!" began the King. "None better . . . "

For the rest of the afternoon, until the potion wore off, Lloyd stood at the end of the King's nose and measured carefully as the King, guided by Grimweed, found all sorts of nice, positive things to say about female members of his staff and family. Gradually, three centimetres at a time, his nose got shorter and shorter.

In the kitchen that evening, Grimweed was just finishing his instructions to King Wo's staff.

"So if it starts to grow again," he was saying, "leave it a couple of days until he's really fed up with it, then give him a small dose of 'Mr Nice Guy' potion. That should do the trick."

"Thank you, Grimweed," said Miriam. "And you, Lloyd. This is going to make our lives a lot more pleasant from now on."

"Don't mention it," replied Grimweed graciously. "Now, if you'll excuse me, there's someone I must say goodbye to."

"Trust you to get a potion involved somewhere!" laughed Gloria.

"'Mr Nice Guy'? Hah! If only! Such a shame it's not permanent!"

"Well," said Grimweed, lowering his voice. "Between you and me, I adapted the recipe just a touch. With every drop of potion he takes, a little bit of the effect stays with him. Gradually he'll become a nicer person!"

"Wow!" said Gloria, with a grin, "so in ten years' time he might be almost bearable!"

"You never know!" laughed Grimweed.

# More Grimfax

This time I thought I'd tell you about some of the other Witches, Wizards and Magical Practitioners who were around in Grimweed's time.

There was Old Wizard Whoops of Wellingburton, who was so called because he kept falling over. His wizard's robe was too long and he kept treading on it, shutting it in doors and suchlike. He was very good at magic remedies for a bruised nose however . . .

The Witch of Grutch was a wart specialist. Unlike most other Wizards and

Witches, she didn't cure them, she grew them. She grew them all shapes and sizes, and was so proud of her work that she would jump out at unsuspecting passers-by and thrust her latest wart under their noses.

"Look!" she would cry. "This one's shaped like a rabbit!" or whatever it was. For some reason people tended to avoid her . . .

Sorceress Sara Tzara, Queen of the Future, specialised in predictions. She was always right. The trouble was that she could only predict uninteresting and unimportant things like: "Tomorrow at three o'clock you will tread on a small piece of cabbage!" Or "By the time you get to market, you will have used the word "fish" fifteen times!" People weren't impressed.

Oh well, that will do for now, see you next time.